Exercise from a Lawn Chair

Frankpage

Frankpage

ATTENTION:
CORPORATIONS, SCHOOLS, GOLF OUTINGS, TENNIS TOURNAMENTS, BOWLING NIGHTS OUT, FRATERNITY AND SORORITY PARTIES, MINOR SURGERIES, WHATEVER . . .

This book is available at a special discount when ordered in bulk quantities. For information, contact: Special Sales Department, Segap Publishing LLC, 6068 S. Apopka-Vineland Road, Orlando, FL 32819

Library of Congress Cataloging-in-Publication Data

Page, Frank L.
Exercise From A Lawn Chair / Frankpage

First Printing
ISBN: 0-9755452-0-5
Library of Congress Control Number: 2004095493

Cover Design: Bill Martini, Martini Graphic Services, Inc.
Printed and bound in the United States of America.

10 9 8 7 6 5 4 3 2 1

Life is too short.

And you are dead too long.

Have fun right now!

– Frankpage

Contents

Who is this Frankpage guy?

Frankpage was born in Pittsburgh, Pennsylvania. He moved to Orlando, Florida, at the age of eight when his parents put him in the back seat of their Dodge station wagon. Back then, they had one of those nifty 3-bench-seaters. The third seat was a fold-down designed so you sat looking out the back of the car. Frankpage has been looking backward ever since.

What's this "Frankpage" stuff? He's been looking at the internet recently and made a discovery. If someone wants to be famous, they really need to have only one name.

For instance, Tigerwoods. Even though he has two names, no one—and I mean no one—calls him by only one of his two names. Seriously, when was the last time you heard anyone call him by his last name? Hey Woods, what'cha doing? Yeah, right. And I've not talked to anyone that knows him well enough to call him by his first name.

If you listen to the television announcers talk about him, it's always Tigerwoods—one word.

There are plenty of celebrities that seem to have lost one of their given names.

Here are some examples:

- When you think about music, you think about Madonna, Cher, Bono.
- When you think about art, you think about Rembrandt, Michelangelo, Renoir.
- When you think about modeling, you think about Fabio, Iman, Frankpage.

OK, maybe you don't *really* think about Frankpage when you think about modeling. But let me tell you that there is at least one person out there that does.

Yep, it's Frankpage himself. Back in seventh grade, he was a tuxedo model in a charity benefit. You know he was stylin' and profilin' even then.

And he wants you to think about Frankpage when you think about exercise gurus, too.

And you should. Frankpage has done his lawn chair research.

i

You Will Love This Book

Sure you will.

You absolutely love the thought of sitting in a lawn chair.

You think exercise just smacks of aerobics. Me too!

And, too much exercise and physical exertion is what might cause you to wake up in the middle of the night. That's not your *and* my kind of healthy.

In this book, you will fine tune your exercise regimen.

You'll become a lean, mean, lawn chair exercising machine.

Blankpage 1

Why This Book is Important to You

Doctors have been telling you for way too long that you should have twenty minutes of exercise three days a week.

Blah, Blah, Blah.

To start with, I'm not a big fan of the word exercise. Three syllables (I don't even like *that* word).

First syllable—ex
Not a positive term.

Second syllable—er
As in a filler word when someone doesn't know what to say.

Third syllable—cise
Trust me, cise doesn't matter.

Put them together and you've got a triple negative that someone shouldn't say and if they do—it just doesn't matter anyway.

Doctors tell us what to do in concept. Anybody (and just about everybody) does that. What they need to tell you is *how* to have fun doing it. And more importantly, show you.

That is why you will love this book. Easy to read. Lots of illustrations. That way you will picture yourself in many situations, getting the supposed exercise you need.

All of that is nice. But, you are a demanding consumer. You need more than nice. You need specific instructions in certain situations. I'm here to help you.

Ever go to a restaurant and quickly decide what you would like to order based on the wonderfully appetizing and mouthwatering description of the food on the menu?

Here's an example:

Cheeseburger and Fries

Ten ounces of Angus beef aged 21 days in our secret aging kitchen. Massage therapists hand rubbed this beef twice a day for tenderness. Grilled to perfection and topped with your choice of cheese (as long as your choice is cheddar).

If you are like me, you are *all over* that cheeseburger.

Here's the tough part—what to drink? Are there times you need help and have to ask your server? Should you have a draft beer? Maybe a bottled beer? How about a mixed drink?

Sometimes you may want to step out on a limb with that burger and have a glass of wine. Where's the wine person? (I don't know, nor can I pronounce, the wine person's official name.)

I've taken all of the beverage stress out of your life with this book. You will know exactly what beverage is recommended for each form of exercise.

Trust me on this; I've done my homework. Your satisfaction is my motivation.

Blankpage 2
(get it?)

iii

What Lawn Chair Should I Buy?

One that fits.

"Really Frankpage, tell me more."

Fits your butt.

And when you find that perfect lawn chair, buy a couple of them. You might want to have different colors for different times of the day.

I do that with my toothbrushes. I use a lighter colored one in the morning and a darker colored one in the evening.

You're thinking, "Thanks for sharing, Frankpage."

Fits the trunk of your car.

Folks can be intimidated by the pressure of scheduling exercise three times a week. Make it easy on yourself. Lawn chairs fold up easily and can be on the go with you.

You never know when someone might call you for an emergency nine holes of Golf from a Lawn Chair.

And what if they said it was time for a quick session of Yoga from a Lawn Chair?

Don't disappoint your friends. Be ready. You'll be glad you did.

Blankpage 3
(you know, one word?)

How to Read This Book

From a lawn chair.

It's time to get in your car.

Drive to the local store and buy a lawn chair.

Now.

Seriously.

Right now.

GO!

Blankpage 4
(stay with me now)

Introduction

We're traveling through another dimension, a dimension not only of sight and sound but of mind. A journey into a wondrous land whose boundaries are that of imagination.

Our next stop, the Lawn Chair Zone.

Here's where you should be thinking, "DO do do do, DO do do do."

Blankpage 5
(No comment at this time)

1

Golf

Here's a great sport if you have all day. My wife thinks golf takes eight hours.

And what a fascinating sport. Most folks drink a bunch of alcoholic beverages—just to warm up. Then they get behind the wheel of a motorized vehicle and drive on the sidewalk. Hey, sounds like fun!

To start the golfing day, you must meet friends for breakfast. Experts say it is the most important meal of the day. I'm sure your stomach will agree. You'll get the most out of your exercise regimen if fully prepared.

Doesn't Frank look healthy? Protein city. Carbs are OK if you are on the extremely modified Atkins-East-Beach-Jared-Subway-Body-For-Half-An-Hour-Abs-For-Ten Minutes-you-name-it-someone-has-written-a-book-about-it-diet (as I am when it suits me.)

Second, you must get a feel for the locker room at the course. A quick hand or two of gin rummy will give you a feel for your post-game environment.

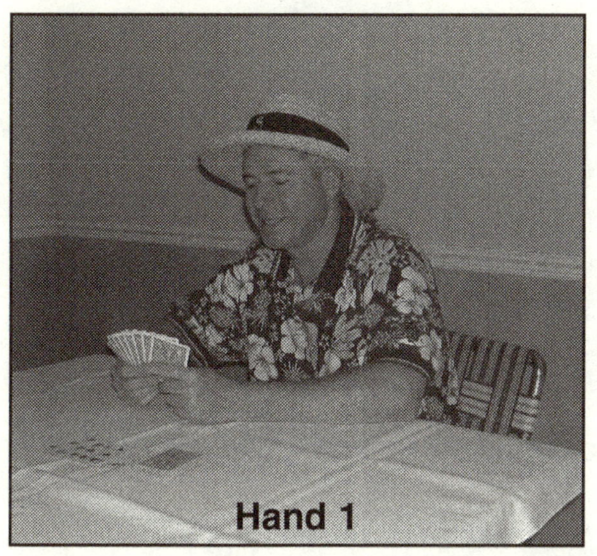

Hand 1

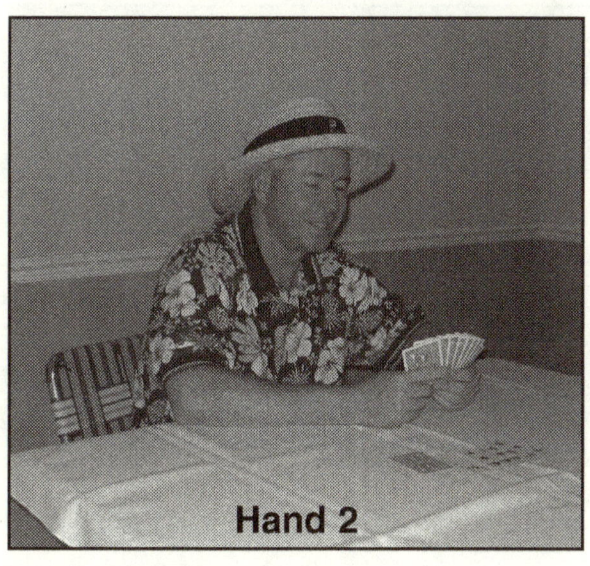

Hand 2

Don't spend a lot of time on the range. Way too much work. Anybody can do that.

Most ranges don't have rough to practice on. When was the last time you spent most of your day in the fairway? Gimme a break.

Don't I look confused being in the fairway?

And what about shrubs to hit out of? Most golfers I know spend a fair amount of time taking free drops from the plants. Can you blame them? I've yet to see a range with enough plants to practice the tough finesse shots needed to round out your golf game.

Seriously, when was the last time you won a trophy for "King of the Range?" Keep those good shots in your pocket for use on the course.

Another helpful tip—take a pile of clubs with you to the golf course. Even though you are not going to use all of them, it's a great idea to take 20 or 25 clubs with you. It's not like you are going to be carrying them on your own. You are going to be in a lawn chair and someone will be proud to hand you whatever club you desire.

Golf bags are plenty big to hold that many. Don't think so? Then go check the bag of any golfer that is retired. It is absolutely immaterial what the "official" rules of golf say the club number limit is. They've got a bazillion clubs in their bag. And they know how to use each and every one of them. The legal ones and the illegal ones.

I play by the PGA rules. That's the Page Golf Association where my motto is, "It's not a law—it's just a rule."

Recommended beverage for Golf from a Lawn Chair

Morning Bloody Mary

Noon Gin and Tonic with a twist

Afternoon Corona with a Lime

(This menu suggestion ensures at least three fruit and vegetable servings per day. Remember—I care deeply about you and your health!)

Blankpage 6
(Is it really?)

2

Bowling

What a great sport for exercising from a lawn chair!

First, you're in an air conditioned building. Temperature controlled for your personal comfort.

Second, the bar is never more than about 30 lanes away.

Third, automatic scoring machines.

Did you know that most of the time the automatic scorer doesn't recognize when your ball went in the gutter, popped out, and knocked down that last pin you needed for a spare.

Good for your scoring. (I know everyone on the planet cares about their bowling score.)

Quick tip. Familiarize yourself quickly with the gutter and scoring system. That, of course, will lower your stress so you can focus on your exercise regimen.

By the way, who wants to carry around a calculator? However, I know an accountant who used to forget his cell phone a lot. So he'd put his pocket calculator on his hip. Real cool, huh?

I like to wear my TV remote on my hip and go into a sports bar. Tell me I'm not the king.

Last, but not least, you don't have to spend much energy to bowl. This allows for a longer exercise session—always a more personally rewarding experience.

Someone told me doctors have verified that endorphins are released during prolonged exercise. You may be thinking, "Are these good endorphins or bad endorphins?" Trust me—no one I know has ever heard of bad endorphins. They must be your friends.

After all, those same doctors have indicated endorphins cause your brain to associate exercise with good feelings—as long as you are in a lawn chair.

It is important to note that if you find you are medically challenged in this area, similar results have been documented by keeping a bucket of beer under your lawn chair.

Here's the final reason why bowling from a lawn chair is awesome exercise. After you roll the ball, IT IS AUTOMATICALLY RETURNED TO YOU!

Recommended beverage for Bowling from a Lawn Chair

Bucket of Miller Lite

Blankpage 7
(Feeling lucky?)

3

Softball

Here's Frankpage giving the other team a little chatter. He loves to say, "Hey, batter, batter, batter . . . swing!" He also impresses the crowd with, "No stick at the plate." And lots of other neat stuff. As the saying goes, "he's got a million of 'em!".

This is an absolutely true story.

After years of thinking I was an athlete —AND I WAS—in my mind, I was invited to play in a fun softball game.

In a prior life, I used to think that winning was important. Intimidating the opponent was a critical part of winning.

Did I tell you that I pitched softball for about twelve years? And could slowpitch a curve ball? It's absolutely true.

So I showed up at the fun game and was assigned third base. Fortunately, I had my lawn chair with me. I planted my lawn chair right next to third base for six innings.

Of course, I did not let the opposing team use my chair. It easily folded up for MY convenience. And you know I looked good sitting in the dugout. No bench for me.

Six innings and not one of the opposing players could hit the ball to me.

And let me tell you why I was a great offensive player.

The key is to find the aggressive player that wants to pinch run for you.

There are two techniques in lawn chair battering. Whoa! Calm down. We are talking about being the batter here.

The critical issue is that you must take your lawn chair to the plate.

The first approach is to actually stand as the pitcher throws the ball to you. This aggressive behavior tends to confuse the opposition.

Additionally, it lessens the chance of them causing your equipment to malfunction. We certainly don't want any Janet Jackson type stuff to happen.

Just a quick note about equipment maintenance . . .

No one can be successful at my exercise program if they don't maintain their lawn chair. I'm a huge fan of WD-40. However, if you are Greek, invest heavily in Windex.

Back to the exercise itself . . .

When you hit the ball, fold up your lawn chair and leisurely stroll toward first base. Upon arriving, unfold your lawn chair and relax.

If this is the fun game of the kind I insist on, your first base coach will pour an ice cold draft beer from the keg located there.

When your teammate up at bat gets a hit, you once again fold your lawn chair and leisurely head to second base. There, you will be greeted by the second base coach—who will pour you another ice cold draft. This time you will have a different flavor.

Obviously, your goal is to get all the way to home plate. There your home plate coach will pour your fourth flavor of the game.

Quite a fun game, huh?

The second batting procedure is a little different. There has to be that competitive former athlete who takes the game just a bit more seriously than needed. He or she is your designated runner after you hit the ball from your lawn chair. You were thinking team comradery all along, weren't you?

Your friend is thrilled to run for you. After all, the first base coach is waiting to pour a cold one.

Number two is my preferred approach to batting. Everybody wins. A frustrated athlete (who needs to own this book but will never grasp the concept) gets rewarded with a cold one at first base. And I also get rewarded at home plate with a cold one.

Recommended beverage for Four Flavor Softball from a Lawn Chair

---

1st base – Bud Light
2rd base – Michelob Light
3rd base – Amstel Light
Home Plate – Sam Adams Lager

(Sam was a brewer, patriot AND a softball player—a fitting tribute to America.)

Blankpage 8
(Intentionally?)

4

Tennis

This sport drives me crazy.

Who came up with the scoring for this? It makes absolutely no sense.

You start with "love." In tennis, "love" is equal to zero. Nothing. Bupkis.

I'm going on record—I love beer. As Tom T. Hall sang in his early 1970's song, "It makes you a jolly good fellow."

Supposedly, tennis was invented in England. Being the master of partial research, I did an in depth survey and I talked with a buddy of mine from England about this. He proudly thinks the English may be responsible for establishing this athletic challenge. And he agrees with me that there is no logic to the scoring system.

There you have it. From now on, when tennis is played, you must refrain from using the word, "love." Instead, you must use the word, "beer."

Let's go farther in the silly scoring system.

Beer, 15, 30, 40, game.

Who decided that the initial scoring should be worth 15? Someone with three hands?

The next score is worth another 15. OK, if the first score is 15, I'll go with the second score as being 15.

Let's go through the scoring once again up through this point. Beer, 15, 30.

Now I'm getting wound up.

Beer, 15, 30, 40, **40? 40!**

Did the inventor suddenly lose one hand? How in the world do you go from beer—add 15, add another 15—and then add only 10?

But it gets worse. Much worse.

Game.

Beer, 15, 30, 40, game.

How much is game? Are we back to 15? Is it 10? Is it only 5?

I looked. Game is not on my calculator. This causes me to tear my hair out.

Speaking of hair, yes, it is true. My favorite TV sitcom is "Everybody Loves Rogaine."

Right now, you are thinking, "Frankpage, that is a pretty funny joke." And you are right. Congratulate yourself.

Now, back to tennis . . .

Tennis is a tough sport. Except for the pros. They've got it easy. When was the last time you saw those professional players on television have to actually bend over to pick up a ball?

They have the kids run back and forth and back and forth to pick up the tennis balls at the end of a score. Notice I didn't say point or points.

15, 10, 5? Oops, there goes more hair.

Remember what we said about that other amazing sport? The ball comes right back to you? The only way that sport could be better is if the tennis kids handed your bowling ball to you—while you are in your lawn chair.

Stick to bowling. Trust me.

Recommended beverage for Tennis from a Lawn Chair

Colt 45 Malt Liquor

Blankpage 9
(Are you ready for a subtle change?)

5

Horseshoes

I love horseshoes! If there was ever a great sport for exercise from a lawn chair—this is the one!

I'm proud to say that in college I was an Intramural horseshoe runner-up. My semi-natural ability at this exciting sport allowed me to perfect my amazing technique in pitching curve balls on the softball field.

Picture a beautiful sunny day. Maybe a cloud or two in the sky. The gang is confused on how to spend time.

You, being the exercise guru, suggest a rousing game of horseshoes. The crowd goes wild. They love you. You are revered.

It's a lot like bowling. And you know how much you are going to like bowling. Remember—throw the ball—and it comes right back to you. No effort needed to find it like that golf stuff. You get all that plus personal contact. Yea.

Throw the horseshoe and someone will be nice enough to throw it back to you. You don't need one of those tennis ball kids.

And don't you just love the sound of solid ringer?

CLINK.

Let's listen to another one.

CLINK.

Brings back those almost-championship memories.

Here's the secret to winning in horseshoes: borrow them from a Clydesdale.

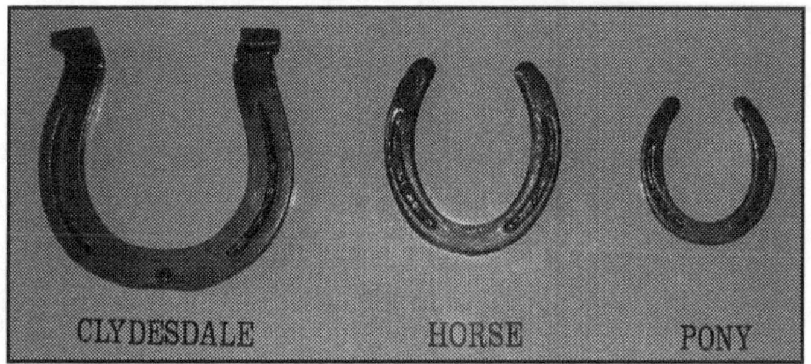

Recommended beverage for Horseshoes from a Lawn Chair

Budweiser (of course)

Track...

OK, if the truth needs to be told, I used to be somewhat of an athlete. Just somewhat.

My senior year in high school, I was on the track team. Ran the 100 and 220. Actually I ran about 180 yards and was heading for the oxygen tent for the last 40.

I was slim back then. Graduated at 5'10" and 125 pounds. That is not a misprint. 125 pounds. My nickname among the other members of our semi-talented team was "the flying toothpick."

There are two distinct things I remember from track. The first is that some high school coaches will teach their kids how to cheat.

Not my coach. He was a great guy. But not much of a track coach. He was the assistant football coach and picked up track to make a few hundred extra dollars.

Anyhow, it was time for the county championship and I was to run against the fastest 220 guy. I was assigned one of the inside lanes—lane 2. Fast Guy was in lane 5—until we began the race. Within twenty-five yards of the start of the race, he had cut over 3 lanes into mine. His coach had taught him to do that. No wonder his times were so good. He'd cut off 10 yards of the race before he'd get back in his lane.

I got him disqualified. Got me moved up from third place to second. Yea me.

My other memory of running was actually the few minutes prior to the start of each race. Picture six kids standing side by side getting ready to run 100 yards down a straightaway. Now take a good look. Yep, there are five athletic looking black guys—and me.

My coach (remember—he's a great guy but not an expert track coach) had not taught me how to run out of the blocks. For those of you that don't know what blocks are, they are the metal things your feet go into to get additional leverage as you start the race. You get very low to the ground and spring out running. They are very legal. In fact, everyone that runs track uses them. I didn't.

There I was having a teammate give me a "foot." If you don't know what that means, the last few paragraphs mean absolutely nothing anyway.

Without exception, one of the black guys would laugh hysterically and ask me "What are you doing?" I would casually respond, "Getting ready to start the race about seven yards behind you."

Then, I'd blow by most of them about two thirds of the way in to the race, and finish my traditional second place. Remember, not really fast. Just somewhat fast. Or, as we still refer to one college fraternity brother, Fairly Fast.

You are now asking, "Frankpage, what direction could this possibly be heading toward Lawn Chairdom?

Beats me. I didn't love track so much. Someone strongly suggested I write a chapter about it. So there you go, someone.

But I love, and so will you, Chapter 6b—

. . . *and Field.*

Recommended beverage for Track . . . from a Lawn Chair

Red Bull and Vodka

(two legal products that do not contain steroids)

6b

...and Field

My personal favorite lawn chair sport of almost all time? . . . *and Field*!

Let your mind run free for one moment (done yet?). Notice that I didn't say, "Think outside of the box." I hate that expression.

First, I'm not a big fan of thinking.

Second, my brain is not shaped like a box. I don't think so anyway. Get it? Don't think.

Again, you are thinking, "Frankpage, that is funny stuff."

Candidly, it is not as funny as something I wrote in the chapter on Tai Chi. But don't skip over there just yet. The chapters are numbered in the order that you should read them.

Don't be thinking outside the book. See, that expression is still stupid when you change it.

While I'm at it, there are a bunch of conference room terms from the 80's and 90's that drive me nuts.

What the hell is a paradigm? I probably didn't even spell it correctly. In a meeting not too long ago, some young overdressed dumbass suggested to a few of us that we "shift our paradigm."

Hey dumbass, shift this.

I should write a few more paragraphs about stupid terms here. In fact……

Sorry to digress. Back to . . . *and Field.*

There are a lot of . . . *and Field* events—events that I wasn't good at so I won't waste your time.

For instance—the high jump. My high school didn't have a foam thing to land on. Just a big old pit of sawdust. Usually damp. Which is probably an appropriate place for a flying toothpick to land.

Picture this for a good time. Run about ten yards. Jump over a bar and walk out looking like the Cowardly Lion from the Wizard of Oz (in the remixed color version.)

The pole vault. Think "I want to run as fast as I can, try and jam a pole into a slot and then be projectiled over a bar and land with a big thud in more damp sawdust"?

Pass.

The shot put. That little metal ball was only the size of a softball, but it was almost ten percent of my entire body weight, soaking wet. Yes, indeed, I was svelte.

Another pass.

There's plenty more . . . *and Field* events that don't matter too much. Let's get to one that does.

Have you ever seen the discus throwers do that crazy spin before they let go of that heavy piece of metal? What's up with that? Who was their high school . . . *and Field* coach?

That's right. Look at the picture. I got rid of the metal thing and got a Frisbee. I can throw it and eventually someone will try and throw it back to me. Someone that understands lawn chair.

Recommended beverage for
. . . and Field from a Lawn Chair

A lot more Red Bull
and Vodka

Hey! Down here!
Blankpage 10

7

White Water Rafting

For some reason, folks seem to think this might be a way to use up a week's vacation. And then they need a week to recover from getting beat up by the rocks when they fall out (and they WILL fall out) of those floating things.

How much fun can it be to ride a roller coaster on water for hours at a time?

Where's the bathroom?

And what are you supposed to eat while you are bobbin' and weavin'?

Haven't these people heard of a cruise ship?

Where's the nightly entertainment?

And the frequent cruisers party?

Where's the waiter with your evening glass of wine?

What about the art auction with the free champagne?

How about the stop for a nap?

How often does the raft stop for an exciting excursion?

And will they hold the raft if you are just a few minutes late from your excursion?

I can't remember the last time I was asked to wear a crash (yes, I said crash) helmet on a cruise ship.

Once again, where's the bathroom?

OK, here's your exercise.

Just go down to your local sports store. They've got rafts—already inflated—ready for you to buy.

Grab your lawn chair and just have a seat in the raft. No up and down. No queasiness. No cold water.

No banging into rocks. Hard rocks. Painful rocks. Rocks that leave memories.

Rocks that leave scars and remove teeth.

Rocks that leave you wondering why you lost your mind and wasted a few days of your vacation in the infirmary.

Hopefully, you are a reformed white water rafter (after reading this). But you probably still need that supposed rush of excitement. Here's what you should do.

When you go to the local sports store with your lawn chair, bring a couple bags of ice. After a few minutes of sitting, just smash the bags of ice into your body for that necessary rush.

Recommended beverage for White Water Rafting from a Lawn Chair

Rolling Rock beer
"33"

Intermission

Ever seen a book with an intermission? Didn't think so. But hey, it's my book, so if it bothers you, write your own!

Bill Martini thought you might like to take a break at this point to help yourself to your favorite beverage.

You should trust Bill. He's the one that designed the cover of this book. If Bill can convince you to BUY THIS BOOK by his awesome cover design, you should trust his judgment on when it is beverage time.

This is what you were really going to do anyway.

And . . . I got an extra four pages in the book this way.

Recommended beverage for Intermission

Metamucil and OJ

8

Famous Lawn Chair Folks

Welcome back.

Hope you enjoyed your (brief) intermission. Don't you wish more writers were sensitive to your personal needs?

Whatever.

Anyhow, who are these famous folks?

Trust me, semi-intense research went into this. Here are three famous lawn chair folks. You'll be as surprised as I was.

Christopher Columbus

That's right—the fellow that discovered America.

Here he is taking a break after landing in the Bahamas. This may be a photo that you haven't seen before.

Yep, Chriscolumbus is chillin' after dropping anchor on the Santa Maria. Most folks didn't realize that Queen Isabella must have been pretty tight with him to provide not one, but three ships that had four pools, seven hot tubs and a dozen or so bars.

Patrick Henry

You may have heard the famous quote. Hopefully, the same way I heard it:

"Give Me Lawn Chair or Give Me Death."

Here's a picture of me looking semi-sincere while impersonating Patrick Henry.

Ok, it's me, Frankpage, in the Press Room of the West Wing in the White House. I needed a way to get this picture in the book.

King Tut

You are now thinking of Steve Martin on Saturday Night Live. Me too. I love that bit.

Steve Martin might have been pictured in this chapter if we had ever met. If I ever see him, I'll ask him.

In the meantime, we need a re-creation of what King Tut actually went through while being carried around.

If you come up with one, send it to me at: kingtut@exercisefromalawnchair.com

We will try to get it in the second printing of this book.

OK, OK, back to exercise.

But of a more individual kind.

You'll love the next chapter on Yoga from a Lawn Chair.

9

Yoga

Who in the world can cross their legs and put their bodies in those wild and crazy contortionists' positions?

And why would anyone think that might be good for you?

Take it from me. Yoga can give you a boo-boo. I know. I was talked into taking a class on a cruise ship last year. And they even charged me $10.00 to be there.

By the way, did you get that yoga and boo-boo joke?

Anyhow, there I am, before breakfast, in a room with fifteen people. All of whom seem to think that 45 minutes of this is better than eating a stack of pancakes at the buffet.

No one told me about the dress code for yoga. Men wearing those silly black stretchy bicycle pants. And those lovely shirts advertising certain companies that must be in the yoga business.

Men doing this. Men. Thinking that they look good in the mirror.

So there I was, stylin' and profilin' in my grey sweatpants and black cotton tee shirt. OK, I was actually advertising a personally signed tee shirt from Carrot Top.

The leader of the class made me attempt to put my body in unnatural positions. Positions that would never be attempted if done correctly from a lawn chair. You will not fall down as I did when you follow my simple directions:

1. Don't go to this class.
2. Follow procedure number one.

Recommended beverage for Yoga from a Lawn Chair

Morning Yoga
Mimosa

Some other time Yoga
Manhattan

10

Pilates

If we are going to talk about yoga, we might as well talk about pilates. I know absolutely nothing about pilates. But here is what I've heard about it.

Pilates comes from the Greek expression, "there's no stuff to sell yogis, so we'll create a need for this big beach ball." Also, the expression, "we'll sell this big beach ball for way too much money."

What's up with that?

Pilates was created for the very impressed with themselves yogis. That is because yoga is just too easy to say.

Say it with me now. "Yo gah."
Say it again. "Yo gah."
And again. "Yo gah." "Yo gah." "Yo gah."
"Yo gah." "Yo gah."

Don't you feel like you are in a scene from Animal House?

Now say, "Pil" "ah" "tees." Doesn't it just get your nose up in the air?

Now say it like you are British. "Oye huf t'go t'muy pil ah tees closs."

Wherever I am in the world right now, I'm laughing because you actually tried to speak like a Brit.

The Brits are probably laughing at you, too.

Recommended beverage for Pilates from a Lawn Chair

Guinness Stout

Blankpage 11
(We’re baaaaack!)

11

Tai Chi

Recently I was on a cruise ship and saw a woman doing some air dancing. But with no music.

No radio.
No boom box.
No one carrying a bad tune.

Didn't get it. For an air guitar, the music comes first.

She was dancing *all by herself.* How much fun could that be?

And she was doing it incorrectly.

How do I know? Two reasons.

First, she fell down. I'm guessing that wasn't planned.

You are thinking rough seas, wind shift, tidal wave. You are guessing wrong. We were docked in Cozumel.

Second, and most important, she wasn't in a lawn chair. That's probably why she fell down. Or maybe she had a boatload (or shipload) to drink. Maybe she was totally shipfaced.

Right now you are thinking, "Frankpage said there was a very funny joke in this chapter and he was absolutely correct. That shipload joke is extremely funny." "And the shipfaced joke—even funnier!"

There you go. Two for the price of one. Anyhow, I'm told Tai Chi can be quite beautiful—if done correctly.

Yawn.

Maybe if you have a good looking lawn chair.

Check the pictures below and you decide.

Recommended beverage for Tai Chi from a Lawn Chair

A shipload of Tsingtao beer.

12

The Next Step

Congratulations to you! You made it all the way this far—through grueling exercise information designed to ensure you become the best you can be.

You are probably looking for a chapter to cool down after all of the hard work. After all, you are on your way toward being a lean, mean exercising from a lawn chair machine.

Maybe a full chapter on stretching would be good at this point.

Maybe not.

Let's talk about stretching.

I just finished another seven night cruise. My waistline is now stretched to the max.

I love cruising! I'd love to go on a seven night cruise once a month. And I would except for one thing. I'd have to have a bellyectomy. Heard those were extremely painful.

And I'm not a big fan of pain. It doesn't take a rocket scientist to know that lawn chairs and pain don't jive.

I strongly recommend a cruise—or two. Want to completely shut down and relax? Want to exercise from a deck chair?

You know you do. And I love you for it.

You are thinking . . . "Frankpage, I've gone this far. Help me to the next level".

My pleasure.

Pick up the phone and call your friendly travel agent. Tell them you've exercised from a lawn chair and you are in desperate need a week of cooldown. Why not, you've earned it.

My current cruise line of preference is Princess. I love cruising with Princess! That's not to say I don't love cruising with other lines.

Frankpagely, (yes, I'll be Frankpage with you) if another cruise line wanted to give me a free cruise, I'd be happy to give them an honest review (a free plug) in my next book. That's assuming the cruise was a good one—and I'm sure it will be. (wink, wink).

If you represent some minor league outfit like Bob's Cruise Line, don't bother to call. I don't (and neither do you) want to be on a rust bucket that someone painted, gave a new name to and said was "refurbished." Trust me, I'll smash a champagne bottle against the side and name it the Garbage Scow.

So, there you go.

You are feeling good.

You are looking fine as wine.

You are ready to make that call to your friendly travel agent.

What are you going to tell them?
Come on—it's easy!

Here's exactly what you are going to say.
Repeat after me. Exactly.

"I am a lean mean lawn chair exercising machine!"

Great job!

Your friendly travel agent will know what to do.

13

Legal Mumbo Jumbo

If you are not a lawyer—good for you! Please keep on reading.

If you are a lawyer and have a good sense of humor—go ahead and continue reading.

If you are a lawyer and are not sure if you have a good sense of humor—you may stop here.

If you are a lawyer and know you don't have a good sense of humor—I should sue you for something silly. Just to keep you busy.

Many exercise books suggest you consult a physician before starting any exercise program. Here's my official disclaimer. "Do what ever you want. I'm just astounded you got this far into this book without throwing it away."

If you don't like my beverage selections, I really don't mind. I don't have a liquor license. You are welcome to consult a qualified bartender. What a great idea. Glad I thought of it.

As in any fine dining restaurant, substitutes are permitted. Frankpagely, I'd be interested in what you might change. Please email me at thirsty@exercisefromalawnchair.com.

A lot of things you read have fine print that is quasi-understandable. Why be different? Our print will be fine. In addition, it will be quasi-understandable.

Here goes . . .

Low gas mileage may be the result of wrong tire pressure. No recovery, no fee. Failure to maintain proper chlorine levels in your swimming pool may result in dirty water. Tomato sauce may cause an outbreak of spagettitis. Beware of sudden undertow. Do not lick the stamps. Professional wrestling may be real. Smoking permitted in Florida if you face east and walk eighty, maybe ninety miles. You should be in international waters by then. Financing based on 18.9% APR. Options include power steering, power brakes, tinted glass, AM-FM-CD, pickles and mustard. Floss daily. Backup your data early and often—just like you vote. Apply ointment to exposed areas only. Allow six to eight weeks for delivery. If you received this via email, delete it immediately. Otherwise, 10,000 spammers will infiltrate your refrigerator. No fishing unless signage otherwise says so. Do not flush the toilet while showering. Speed of light may vary at night. Speed limits strictly enforced. Check with your city or county government for submarine racing license. Record frequencies at proper volume. Do not sit or lean on pool table. Legal pads may be illegal in some states. There once was a man from Nantucket. Webster's New Collegiate Dictionary has been deemed appropriate in high school. No paper was injured during the die-cut. Shaken not stirred. Contains sulfites. Does anybody really know what time it is? Contains SPF 147 as a time released ingredient. Consult your doctor before playing bingo. Apply generously and evenly but not everywhere all at once. Congratulations! Mutual funds are not mutually exclusive. Order before midnight tonight. Wine glasses may be 20/20. The internet phone book has just arrived. One entry per entrant. And finally—Actual results may vary!

Blankpage 12
(Think this is the last one?)

A lot of people helped with this book. You are thinking, "No kidding, Frankpage. You couldn't have done this all by yourself!"

So here's where I thank a bunch of folks you probably don't know. Or do you? As they (by the way, who is the infamous "they"?) say in a beauty pageant—"In no particular order . . .

Three of the funniest stand-up comedians I've ever seen. Ronniebullard, Dougdoane and Russnagel. If they visit your town, make sure you see them perform. I've seen or worked with hundreds and hundreds of comics. These guys are three of the best.

Noted authors Tobyunwin and Eliportnoy. You should consider buying their books.

Dougcolson and the spectacular folks at Conway's BBQ.

Cynthiaandjayjohnson of Lake Fairview Marina.

Helenandchrischristini.

Larryanddarleneumstadter,
Bruceandnancywalton,
Joanandrichardcoppedge,
Judyandjimdeaton,
Royandestherbeckett.

MaryrecchiaandBobbrown,
Mikehardiman and Massage therapist extraordinaire Peekerclemins.

Nancyandtonygreenfield,
Annandfredconley,
Micheleandjeffkohl,
Sueandjerryroberts,
Jimanddiannepage,
Tompageanddonnasimmerson.

Ronbaker, Pauldunn, Ricpayne and Shannonvincent.

The awesome team at Caribbean Soul.

The Amazing Earl. He knows his last name. You don't really care do you? You do? OK, it's Ratliff. Yep, he's The Amazing Earlratliff. It's good being Earl.

Billandjoemartini and the incredibly talented team at Martini Graphic Services, Inc., in Orlando, Florida.

And, of course, the lady that causes me to smile EVERY day of my life—my wife Jackie. You should meet her. You will smile, too!

Blankpage 14
(Superstitious?)

About the Author

Frank Page has entertained for corporations and at conventions with his stand up comedy routine, “DebitMan” for over 15 years. He has actually performed for the IRS!

A certified public accountant for 25 years, he is President of Business Development Partners, Inc. in Orlando, Florida.

Additionally, he is a licensed auctioneer in central Florida and the owner of Prime Auctioneers, Inc.

DebitMan runs a clean show, suitable for a variety of audiences. His brand of humor, presentation and delivery is particularly enjoyed by business groups.

Please visit him at www.debitman.tv.

Blankpage xv
(thanks for noticing!)

www.ingramcontent.com/pod-product-compliance
Lightning Source LLC
LaVergne TN
LVHW091012080826
845145LV00003B/1233

* 9 7 8 0 9 7 5 5 4 5 2 0 1 *